KU-793-146

This book belongs to

_____

_____

**For**
**Simon, Bobbin and Tess**

First
published in
Great Britain 1998
by Egmont UK Limited
The Yellow Building,
1 Nicholas Road,
London W11 4AN
www.egmont.co.uk

Text and
illustrations
copyright © Lydia
Monks 1998
Lydia Monks has
asserted her moral
rights

A CIP
catalogue record
for this title is available
from The British Library.
ISBN 978 1 4052 1246 5

Stay safe online. Egmont
is not responsible for
content hosted by
third parties.

All rights
reserved. No part
of this publication may
be reproduced, stored in a
retrieval system, or transmitted,
in any form or by any means,
electronic, mechanical,
photocopying, recording or
otherwise, without the prior
permission of the publisher
and copyright
owner

Lydia Monks

# I Wish I Were a Dog

EGMONT

I wish I were a dog.
Dogs have all the fun.

Dogs can play
in the park.

Dogs can howl and bark.

They can chase robbers.

They can even be film stars.

I'm fed up!
I wish I were a dog!

**Don't be silly, Kitty.**
**Sometimes dogs are stupid!**

They chew old bones.

They're made to do tricks.

They're put on leads,

and have to do as they're told.

**Cats can do lots of things.**
**Cats are clever.**

Cats catch mice.

They can see in the dark,

and move without a sound.

Cats jump high and

cats climb trees.

They can prowl like tigers

and come and go as they please.

And, of course,
cats can sleep anywhere!

So you see, you are very special
just as you are!

I wish I were a cat!

# More great picture books...

Meet Babbit, a toy bunny who has a startling adventure – that he can't stop rabbiting on about!